*A Weird Tale
and Other Supernatural Stories*

By William Q. Judge

ISBN: 978-1-63118-518-2

Esoteric Classics:
Occult Fiction

Other Books in this Series and Related Titles

Audio versions are also available on Audible, Amazon and Apple

Other Books in this Series and Related Titles

Paracelsus, the Four Elements and Their Spirits by M P Hall (978-1-63118-400-0)

The Alchemical Catechism of Paracelsus by Paracelsus (978-1-63118-513-7)

Freher's Process in the Philosophical Work by D A Freher (978-1-63118-484-0)

The Magician's Heavenly Chaos by Thomas Vaughan (978-1-63118-500-7)

Masonic and Rosicrucian History by M P Hall & H Voorhis (978-1-63118-486-4)

Tao Te Ching & Commentary by Lao Tzu & C Johnston (978-1-63118-495-6)

The Life of Pythagoras by Porphyry (978-1-63118-512-0)

The Influence of Pythagoras on Freemasonry and Other Essays (978-1-63118-404-8)

The Golden Verses of Pythagoras: Five Translations (978-1-63118-479-6)

On the Philadelphian Gold by Philochrysus & Philadelphus (978-1-63118-511-3)

Book of Vexations by Paracelsus (978-1-63118-520-5)

A Collection of Early Writings on Astral Travel (978-1-63118-477-2)

The Secret Book of the Philosopher's Stone by Artephius (978-1-63118-517-5)

The Old Past Master by Carl H Claudy (978-1-63118-464-2)

The Path of Light: A Manual of Maha-Yana Buddhism (978-1-63118-471-0)

The Hymns of Hermes by G. R. S. Mead (978-1-63118-405-5)

Clairvoyance and Psychic Abilities by Leadbeater & Besant (978-1-63118-403-1)

Ancient Mysteries and Secret Societies by M P Hall (978-1-63118-410-9)

*A Collection of Writings Related to Occult, Esoteric, Rosicrucian and Hermetic Literature,
Including Freemasonry, the Kabbalah, the Tarot, Alchemy and Theosophy*
various authors *Volumes 1-4*
(978-1-63118-713-1) (978-1-63118-714-8)
(978-1-63118-715-5) (978-1-63118-716-2)

Audio Versions are also available on Audible, Amazon and Apple

Table of Contents

INTRODUCTION

The word "esoteric" can be difficult to define. Esotericism in general can be seen less as a system of beliefs and more as a category, which encompasses numerous, different systems of beliefs. It's a bit of juxtaposition, since the word "esoteric" indicates something that few people know about, while the term itself broadly covers numerous philosophies, practices, areas of study and belief systems.

In a greater sense, Esotericism acts as a storehouse for secret knowledge, which is often considered ancient (by *tradition, if not by fact)*, passed down from generation to generation, in private. At various times in history, simply possessing the knowledge of some of these subjects, was considered illegal and a jailable offence, if discovered. This usually included such general topics as Alchemy, Qabalah, Hermeticism, Occultism, Ceremonial Magic, Astrology, Divination, Rosicrucianism and so on. Collectively, these areas of study were often referred to as the esoteric sciences.

Sometimes, the outer garment of a subject isn't esoteric, while what is hidden beneath it, is. As an example, Freemasonry isn't necessarily esoteric by nature (at *least not anymore),* but certain signs, passwords and handshakes given to the candidate during their initiation, are in fact, esoteric, in the sense that they are hidden from the general public.

Today, in the twenty-first century, such topics are readily available at bookstores across the country, and numerous mainsteam publishers offer beginners guides and coffee-table volumes on many of these subjects, intended for mass appeal. Books like *"The Secret"* have turned previously arcane topics into household knowledge. All that being the case, however, it isn't to say that there still aren't buried secrets to uncover, ancient wisdom being ignored and forgotten mysteries to be explored. In fact, it is often that we are only able to further our own studies by standing on the shoulders of these disappearing giants.

Lamp of Trismegistus is doing its part to help preserve humanity's esoteric history by making some of these classics available to those students who are seeking to unearth the knowledge of these ancient colossi.

So, be sure to check out other titles in our *Esoteric Classics* series, as well as our *Foundations of Freemasonry Series, Theosophical Classics, Occult Fiction, Paranormal Research Series, Esoteric Classics, Supernatural Fiction, Studies in Buddhism* and our *Christian Apocrypha Series* as well as numerous other subjects. You can also download the audio versions of many of these titles from iTunes or Audible, for learning on the go.

A WEIRD TALE

PART I

The readers of this magazine have read in its pages, narratives far more curious and taxing to belief than the one I am about to give fragments of. The extraordinary Russian tale of the adept at the rich man's castle when the infant assumed the appearance of an old man will not be forgotten. But the present tale, while not in the writer's opinion containing anything extremely new, differs from many others in that I shall relate some things, I myself saw. At this time too, the relation is not inopportune, and perhaps some things here set down may become, for many, explanations of various curious occurrences during the past five years in India and Europe.

To begin with, this partial story is written in accordance with a direction received from a source which I cannot disobey and in that alone must possess interest, because we are led to speculate why it is needed now.

Nearly all of my friends in India and Europe are aware that I have travelled often to the northern part of the South American continent and also to Mexico. That fact has been indeed noticed in this magazine. One very warm day in July 1881, I was standing at the vestibule of the Church of St. Theresa in the City of Caracas, Venezuela. This town was settled by the Spaniards who invaded Peru and Mexico and contains a Spanish-speaking people. A great crowd of people were at the door and just then a procession emerged with a small boy running ahead and clapping a loud clapper to frighten away the devil. As I noticed this, a voice in English said to me "curious that they have preserved that singular ancient custom." Turning I saw a remarkable looking old man who smiled peculiarly and said, "come with me and have a talk." I complied and he soon led me to a house which I had often noticed, over the door being a curious old Sanish tablet devoting the place to the patronage of St. Joseph and Mary. On his invitation I entered and at once saw that here was not an ordinary Caracas house. Instead of lazy dirty Venezuelan servants, there were only clean Hindoos such as I had often seen in the neighbouring English Island of Trinidad; in the place of the disagreeable fumes of garlic and other things usual in the town, there hung in the air the delightful perfumes known only to the Easterns. So I at once concluded that I had come across a delightful adventure.

Seating ourselves in a room hung with tapestry and cooled by waving punkahs that evidently had not been long put up, we engaged in conversation. I tried to find out who this man was, but he evaded me. Although he would not admit or deny knowledge of the Theosophical Society of Madame Blavatsky or of the Mahatmas, he constantly made such references that I was sure he knew all about them and had approached me at the church designedly. After quite a long talk during which I saw he was watching me and felt the influence of his eye, he said that he had liberty to explain a little as we had become sufficiently acquainted. It was not pleasure nor profit that called him there, but duty alone. I referred to the subterranean passages said to exist in Peru full of treasure and then he said the story was true and his presence there connected with it. Those passages extended up from Peru as far as Caracas where we then were. In Peru they were hidden and obstructed beyond man's power to get them but in this place the entrances were not as well guarded although in 1812 an awful earthquake had levelled much of the town. The Venezuelans were rapacious and these men in India who knew the secret had sent him there to prevent any one finding the entrances. At certain seasons only there were possibilities of discovery; the seasons over he could depart in security, as until the period came again no one could find the openings without the help and consent of the adepts. Just then a curious bell sound broke on the air and he begged me to remain until he returned as he was called, and then left the room. I waited a long time filled with speculations, and as it was getting late and past dinner hour I was about to leave. Just as I did so a Hindoo servant quickly entered and stood in front of the only door. As he stood there I heard a voice say as if through a long pipe: "Stir not yet." Reseating myself, I saw that on the wall, where I had not before noticed it, hung a curious broad silver plate brightly shining. The hour of the day had come when the sun's light struck this plate and I saw that on it were figures which I could not decipher. Accidentally looking at the opposite wall, I saw that the plate threw a reflection there upon a surface evidently prepared for that purpose and there was reproduced the whole surface of the plate. It was a diagram with compass, sign and curious marks. I went closer to examine, but just at that moment the sun dipped behind the houses and the figures were lost. All I could make out was that the letters looked like exaggerated Tamil or Telugu — perhaps Zend. Another faint bell sounded and the old man returned. He apologized, saying he had been far away, but that we would meet again. I asked where, and he said, "In London." Promising to return I hurried away. Next day I could not find him at all and discovered that there were two houses devoted to Joseph and Mary and I could not tell which I had seen him in. But in each I found Spaniards, Spanish servants and Spanish smells.

In 1884 I went to London and had forgotten the adventure. One day I strolled into an old alley to examine the old Roman wall in the Strand which is said to be 2,000 years old. As I entered and gazed at the work, I perceived a man of foreign aspect there who looked at me as I entered. I felt as if he knew me or that I had met him, but was utterly unable to be sure. His eyes did not seem to belong to his body and his appearance was at once startling and attractive. He spoke to the attendant, but his voice did not help me. Then the attendant went out and he approaching me, said:

"Have you forgotten the house of Joseph and Mary?" In a moment I knew the expression that looked out through those windows of the soul, but still this was not the same man. Determined to give him no satisfaction I simply said, "no," and waited.

"Did you succeed in making out the reflection from the silver plate on the wall?" Here was complete identification of place, but not of person.

"Well," I said, "I saw your eyes in Caracas but not 'your body,' He then laughed and said, "I forgot that, I am the same man, but I have borrowed this body for the present and must indeed use it for some time, but I find it pretty hard work to control it. It is not quite "to my liking. The expression of my eyes of course you knew, but I lost sight of the fact that you looked at the body with ordinary eyes."

Once more I accompanied him to his residence and when not thinking of his person but only listening with the soul, I forgot the change. Yet it was ever present, and he kindly gave me an account of some things connected with himself, of absorbing interest. He began in this way.

"I was allowing myself to deceive myself, forgetting the Bhagavat Gita where it tells us, that a man is his soul's friend and his soul's enemy, in that retreat in Northern India where I had spent many years. But the chance again arose to retrieve the loss incurred by that and I was given the choice of assuming this body."

At this point again I heard the signal bell and he again left me. When he returned, he resumed the story.

If I can soon again get the opportunity, I will describe that scene, but for the present must here take a halt.

PART II

There are many who cannot believe that I have been prevented from writing the whole of this tale at once, and they have smiled when they read that I would continue it "if allowed." But all who know me well will feel that there is some truth in my statement. It may interest those who can read between the lines to know that I attempted several times to finish the tale so as to send it all in one batch to the magazine, but always found that at the point where the first chapter ends my eyes would blur, or the notes ready for the work became simply nonsense, or some other difficulty intervened, so that I was never until now able to get any further with it than the last instalment. It is quite evident to me that it will not be finished, although I know quite well what it is that I have to say. This part must, therefore, be the last, as in trying to reach a conclusion much time is wasted in fighting against whatever it is that desires to prevent my going into full details. In order then to be able to get out even so much as this I am compelled to omit many incidents which would perhaps be interesting to several persons; but I shall try to remember particularly and relate what things of a philosophical nature were repeated to me.

As I sat there waiting for the host to come back, I felt the moral influence of another mind, like a cool breeze blowing from a mountain. It was the mind of one who had arrived at least at that point where he desired no other thing than that which Karma may bring, and, even as that influence crept over me, I began to hear a voice speaking as it were through a pipe the end of which was in my head, but which stretched an immense distance into space making the voice sound faint and far off. It said:

"The man whose passions enter his heart as waters run into the unswelling passive ocean obtaineth happiness; not he who lusteth in his lusts. The man who having abandoned the lusts of the flesh worketh without inordinate desires, unassuming, and free from pride, obtaineth happiness. This is divine dependence. A man being possessed of this confidence in the Supreme goeth not astray: even at the hour of death should he attain it he shall mix with the incorporeal nature of Brahm. He who enjoyeth the *Amreeta* that is left of his offerings obtaineth the eternal spirit of Brahm the Supreme."

The atmosphere of the room seemed to give the memory great retentive power, and when on returning to my room that night I fell upon those sentences in the Bhagavat Gita. I knew that they had come to me from a place or a person for whom I should have respect.

Occupied with such thoughts, I did not notice that my host had returned, and looking up was somewhat startled to see him sitting at the other side of the apartment reading a book. The English clothes were gone and a white Indian dhoti covered him, and I could see that he wore round his body the Brahmanical cord. For some reason or other he had hanging from a chain around his neck an ornament which, if it was not Rosicrucian, was certainly ancient.

Then I noticed another change. There seemed to have come in with him, though not by the door, other visitors which were not human. At first I could not see them, though I was aware of their presence, and after a few moments I knew that whatever they were they rushed hither and thither about the room as if without purpose. They had yet no form. This absorbed me again so that I said nothing and my host was also silent. In a few more moments these rushing visitors had taken from the atmosphere enough material to enable them to become partly visible. Now and then they made a ripple in the air as if they disturbed the medium in which they moved about, just as the fin of a fish troubles the surface of the water. I began to think of the elemental shapes we read of in Bulwer Lytton's Zanoni, and which have been illustrated in Henry Kunrath's curious book on the Cabala of the Hebrews.

"Well," said my strange friend, "do you see them? You need have no fear, as they are harmless. They do not see you, excepting one that appears to know you. I was called out so as to try if it were possible for you to see them, and am glad that you do."

"And the one that knows me," said I. "Can you identify it in any way?"

"Well," said he, "let us call it *he*. He seems to have seen you — been impressed with your image just as a photograph is on a plate — somewhere or other, and I also see that he is connected with you by a name. Yes, it is —— ."

And then he mentioned the name of an alleged elemental or nature spirit which at one time, some years ago, was heard of in New York.

"He is looking at you now, and seems to be seeking something. What did you have or make once that he knew of?"

I then recollected a certain picture, a copy of an Egyptian papyrus of the Hall of Two Truths showing the *trial of the Dead,* and so replied, regretting that I had not got it with me to show my friend. But even as I said that, I saw the very picture lying upon the table. Where it came from I do not know, as I had no recollection of bringing it with me. However, I asked no questions, and waited, as my host was looking intently at the space above my head.

"Ah, that is what he was looking for, and he seems to be quite pleased," he said, as if I could hear and see just as he did. I knew he referred to the elemental.

In another moment my attention was rivetted on the picture. Its surface bobbed up and down as if waves ran over it, and crackling sounds rose from every part. They grew louder and the motion ceased, while from a certain point arose a thin whitish vapor that wavered unsteadily to and fro. Meanwhile the strange visitors I have mentioned seemed to rush about more in the vicinity of the paper, while now and again one of them took what looked like a flying leap from one end of the room to the other, with a queer faint boom of a metallic character following his rapid motion.

Here I must draw the veil unwillingly. Let me violate the unities and the frame of this tale by just putting down a few sentences, leaving it to the imagination to draw inferences.

"Those strange delineations of form? Quite easily. They were seen by the seeresses in the temple, It is quite true that elementals have no form as such . . . But there are undoubtedly types, and [those] Egyptians were not the men to do anything unscientifically . . . There is an occult reason why, although without form, these particular shapes were assumed. And having been once assumed and seen thus by the seer, they always repeated that form to those persons. So the representative of the astral light or of wisdom or the recording angel, is yellow in color, very tall, with a long bill like a stork. Or the one who takes the weight of the soul is always seen with a jackal's head. . . . No, there is no prohibition against telling the occult reason. It is merely this: were it told, only one in a thousand hearers would see any meaning or reason in it. . . . Let your mind reflect also upon the peculiarity that all the judges sitting above there have heads alike, while in color they differ, each one having a feather, the emblem of truth, on his head . . . No, it is not Hindu, and yet it is the same. They used to say, and I think you may find it in one of their books, that everything is in the Supreme soul, and the Supreme soul in everything." [Bhagavad-Gita] So the great truth

16

is one, while it can be seen in a thousand different ways. We [Egyptians] took a certain view and made every symbol consistent and of a class consonant with our view. . . . And just as the Hindus are accused of being idolaters because they have represented Krishna with eight arms standing on the great elephant, we, who did not picture an eight-armed divinity, are charged with having worshipped jackals, cats and birds . . . "Yes, it is a pity, but the sand that buries Egypt has not been able to smother the great voice of that sphinx, the *esoteric doctrine*. But not through us except in some such manner as this, now and then. In India the light burns, and in a living people still resides the key — ."

Just then the bobbing of the picture began again and the same whitish column wavered over it. The faint boom of the airy elementals recommenced, and again claimed my attention, and then the picture was still.

I may say that the whole of the conversation has not been given. It is not necessary that it should be. My host had maintained perfect silence all the while, and seemed to await my voice, so I said:

"What could have induced you to leave those peaceful places where true progress may be gained."

"Well," he replied, "very likely they were peaceful, and quite truly progress was possible, but you do not appreciate the dangers also. You have read *Zanoni*, and perhaps have an exaggerated idea of the horrible *Dweller of the Threshold*, making of her a real person or thing. But the reality is much worse. When you get into what you have called the 'peaceful places,' this power becomes tenfold stronger than it is found to be on the plane in which we now live in London."

"Why, I supposed that there, free from the cankering anxieties of modern life, the neophyte sailed happily on through plain seas to the shores of the fortunate isles."

"Far from that. On that plane it is found that, although from the spiritual sun there falls upon us the benign influence of those great sages who, entering paranirvana, throw off their accumulated goodness for our benefit, the evil influence that is focussed by the dark side of the moon falls as well, and with its power undiminished. The little temptations and difficulties of your life are as nothing compared to that struggle for then it is realized that the self is the enemy of the self, as well as its friend."

"But," said I, "was the fault committed a great one, that it should condemn you to this task?"

"No, not great as you term it. But quite great enough; and in consequence I had to take my choice. In Caracas you saw me as an illusion of a certain character. There I did what was required, the illusion being perfect except as to the eyes. Now you see another illusion, and yet at the same time a reality such as is connoted by that word when used by modern scientists. It is a body that lives and will die. The Karma is hard perhaps, but I grumble not. But is it not an illusion in every sense when you know that although this body speaks and thinks, still, I the speaker am not visible to you?"

These words are not mine. If some of them seem meaningless or queer to many readers, do not blame the writer. There are those who can understand. There are yet others who have latent thoughts that need but these words to call them into life. I cannot give any greater detail than the above as to himself, because he had reasons for preventing me, although he might perhaps, himself tell more to another.

One curious thing of interest he said, which will furnish some with food for thought. It was when I referred to the use of the body he had, so to say, *borrowed,* that he said:

"Don't you know that many experiments are possible in that way, and that some students are taught peculiarly? I have stood aside from this earthly tabernacle many a time to let in those who, notwithstanding that they operated the machine well enough and made quite a respectable use of it, did not know what they did. They were, if you like, dreaming. While here, in this body, they were essentially it, for the time speaking its words, thinking its thoughts and not able to control it. Not desiring to in fact, because they were completely identified with it. When they waked up in their own apartments either a singular dream whispered a fragmentary song through their brain, or they retained no remembrances; whatever of it. In such a case the body, being really master, might do or say that which I would not — or the occupier, temporarily strong, might say out of real recollection things having relation only to that life of which his hearers would have no knowledge."

Just then some clock struck. The atmosphere seemed to clear itself. A strange and yet not unfamiliar perfume floated through the room, and my host said, "Yes, I will show you a verse someone tells me to show you."

He walked over to the table, took up a queer little book printed in Sanskrit, yellow with age and seeming to have been much used. Opening it he read:

"This supreme spirit and incorruptible Being, even when it is in the body, neither acteth, nor is it affected, because its nature is without beginning and without quality. As the all-moving Akas, or ether, from the minuteness of its parts, passeth everywhere unaffected, even so the Omnipresent spirit remaineth in the body unaffected. As a single sun illumines the whole world, even so doth the

spirit enlighten every body. They who, with the eye of wisdom, perceive the body and the spirit to be thus distinct, and that there is a final release from the animal nature, go to the Supreme."— Bhagavad Gita.

A CURIOUS TALE

Some years ago I ran down to the Lakes of Killarney, but not for the purpose merely of seeing them as any other traveler. During my boyhood the idea of going there had always been before me, and, in dreams I would often find myself on the water or wandering nearby. After this had occurred many times, I procured photographs of the scenery and was quite surprised to find that the dreams were accurate enough to seem like recollections. But various vicissitudes took me to other parts of the world, so that I had passed my majority without having visited the place, and, indeed, the decision to go there at last was not made until one day, while looking into a shop window in Dublin, my eye fell upon a picture of Killarney, and in an instant I was filled with a strong desire to see them. So I went on the first train and was very soon there, quartered with an old man who from the first seemed like an old friend.

The next day or two were devoted to wandering about with no purpose nor with very great satisfaction, for the place as a bit of country did not interest me after all my wanderings in many different climes. But on the third day I went off into a field not far from the shores of one of the sheets of water, and sat down near an old well. It was still early in the afternoon, and unusually pleasant. My mind had no particular object before it, and I noticed an inability, quite unusual, to follow long a definite train of thought. As I sat thus, drowsiness came over my senses, the field and the well grew grey but still remained in sight, yet I seemed to be changing into another man, and, as the minutes flew by, I saw the shadowy form or picture of a tall round tower rising, some fifty feet high, just beyond the well. Shaking myself, this disappeared and I thought I had fought off the sleepy feeling, but only for a moment. It returned with new intensity.

The well had disappeared and a building occupied its place, while the tall tower had grown solid; and then all desire to remain myself disappeared. I rose with a mechanical feeling that my duty, somehow or other, called me to the tower, and walked over into the building through which I knew it was necessary to go in order to reach the tower. As I passed inside the wall, there was the old well I had seen upon first coming into the field, but the strange incident did not attract my attention, for I knew the well as an old landmark. Reaching the tower, the steps wound up before me to the top, and as I mounted them a voice quite familiar called my name — a name not the same that I owned to upon sitting down near the well, but that did not attract my attention any more than the old well inside the wall. At last I emerged upon the top of the tower, and there was an old man keeping up a fire. It was the eternal fire never yet known to have gone out, and I out of all the other young disciples alone was permitted to help the old man.

As my head rose above the level of the low rim of the tower, I saw a calm and beautiful mountain not far away, and other towers nearer to it than mine.

"You are late," said the old man. I made no reply, as there was none to make; but I approached and showed by my attitude that I was ready to go on watching in his place. As I did this it flashed across me that the sun was nearing the horizon, and for an instant the memory of the old man with whom I had lodged came before me, as well as the express train to be reached by cart, but that faded out as the old watcher looked into my brain with his piercing eyes.

"I fear to leave you in charge," was his first remark. "There is a shadow, dark and silent, near you."

"Do not fear, father," said I; "I will not leave the fire nor permit it to go out." "If you do, then our doom is sealed and the destiny of Innisfallen delayed."

With those words he turned and left me, and soon I heard his foot-fall no more on the winding stairs that led below.

The fire seemed bewitched. It would hardly burn, and once or twice it almost paralyzed me with fear, so nearly did it expire. When the old man left me, it was burning brightly. At last it seemed that my efforts and prayers were successful; the blaze sprang up and all looked well. Just then a noise on the stairs caused me to turn round, and to my surprise a complete stranger came upon the platform where none but the guardians were allowed.

"Look," said he; "those fires beyond are dying out."

I looked and was filled with fear to see that the smoke from the towers near the mountain had died out, and in my sudden amazement rushed to the parapet to get a nearer view. Satisfied that what the stranger said was true, I turned to resume my watch, and there, O horror! my own fire was just expiring. No lights or tinder were permitted there; the watcher had to renew the fire by means of the fire. In a frenzy of fear I leaped to new fuel and put it on the fire, fanned it, laid my face to it and strove with maddened gasps to blow the flame up, but all my efforts were vain, — it was dead.

A sickening dread seized me, succeeded by a paralysis of every nerve except those that aid the hearing. I heard the stranger move toward me, and then I recognized his voice as he spoke. No other noises were about, all was dead and cold, and I seemed to know that the ancient guardian of the fire would return no more, that no one would return, that some calamity had fallen.

"It is the past," the stranger began. "You have just reached a point where you failed to feed the fire ages ago. It is done. Do you want to hear of these things? The old man has gone long ago, and can trouble you no more. Very soon you will be again in the whirl of the nineteenth century."

Speech then returned to me and I said, "Yes, tell me what this is, or has been."

"This is an old tower used by the immediate descendants of the white Magicians who settled on Ireland when England's Isle had not arisen from the sea. When the great Masters had to go away, strict injunctions were left that no fires on these towers were to go out, and the warning was also given that, if the duties of life were neglected, if charity, duty, and virtue were forgotten, the power to keep these fires alive would gradually disappear. The decadence of the virtues would coincide with the failure of the fires, and this, the last tower, guarded by an old and young man, would be the last to fail, and that even it could save the rest if its watchers were faithful.

"Many years elapsed, and the brilliant gem placed upon the mount of Innisfallen blazed both by day and night until at last it seemed to fade a little. The curious sounding-stones, now found in Ireland, were not so easily blown; only when a pure and faithful servant came down from the White Tower did the long, strange, and moving sounds float over the mountains from the stone placed near the mount on which was the gem. Those stones had been used by the great magicians, and when the largest of them all, lying near the great White Tower, was sounded, the fairies of the lakes appeared; when the stone of the mount was blown together with that at the White Tower, the spirits of the air and the water ranged themselves obediently around.

"But all this altered, and unbelief crept in while the fires were kept up as a form.

"You were relied on with the old man. But vain dreams detained you *one* hour beyond your appointed time on this fatal day, now in the past but shown you by my special favour. You came, but late. The old man was compelled to wait, but still feared to leave you, for he saw with prescient eye the dark finger of fate. He descended the stairs, and at its foot fell down and died. Your curiosity then drew you at the exact fatal moment to look at yonder tower, although you knew the prophecy and believed it. That moment decided all — and, poor boy, you could not hold back the iron hand of destiny.

"The fire has gone out. You returned to the floors below; at the foot of the stairs you saw them carrying off the old man and —— ** "

At this point I saw the shadowy, waving shape of the tower the building had disappeared, the well was beside me, and I was in the field again. Oh!

THE SERPENT'S BLOOD

It was an old and magic island. Many centuries before, the great good Adepts had landed on its shores from the West and established for a while the Truth. But even they could not stay the relentless tread of fate, and knew that this was only a halting place, a spot where should be concentrated spiritual power sufficiently strong to remain as a leaven for several cycles, and that should be a base upon which in long ages after ages might be erected again the spiritual temple of truth. These blessed beings remained there for centuries uncounted, and saw arise out of the adjoining seas other lands, first of soft mud that afterwards hardened into rocks and earth. They taught the people and found them apt students, and from their number drew many disciples who were full of zeal as well as patience and faith. Among the least of those I was, and toiled long and earnestly through successive lives upon the Island. And the Island came to be known as the Isle of Destiny, from mysterious future events foretold for it by the greatest of the Adepts and their seers.

Yet I succeeded not in reaching the point when I could hope to pass on from the Island with the teachers, who said that at a certain day they must travel away to other lands, leaving behind them their blessing to those who willingly remained of the disciples; those who rebelled had still to remain, but without the aid and comfort of the benediction of the blessed ones.

At last the day of separation came and the kingly guides departed, leaving well established the true religion and practice. Yet we all knew that even that must have its decay, in which perhaps even some of us might have a hand, but the centre of power was not to depart from the Island until its destiny should be accomplished; the power might be hidden, but it would remain latent until the time arrived.

Many years came and went; still I found myself upon the Island again and again reincarnated. With sorrow I saw the ancient practices overlooked and different views prevailing. It was the power of the serpent.

On one well known mountain the Masters had placed a gem, and at the mountain's base a tower. These I have spoken of incidentally in a former tale. I knew that mountain well, and saw it every day from the tower at some distance away where my own duties lay. I was present when the wonderful gem was placed upon the mountain, and of all those who saw the grand event, I alone remembered. Since that day many centuries had rolled away, and the other disciples, reincarnated there also, had forgotten the event but knew of the gem. Some of them who in other lives had been my servants in the tower were now my earthly superiors because they had devoted their minds to formal outward power, which is only the weak symbol of the reality that should exist within. And so the tradition alone remained, but the diamond now blazed less brilliantly than in the days when I first knew it. By night its rays shot up into the heavens, and the priests month after month tried ceremonies and prayers in vain, in order to cause it to burst forth in all the glory of its pristine days. They knew that such a blaze was a possibility — indeed an old prophecy — but that was all they could tell, and were ignorant of the remainder of it, which, if they had known, perhaps none of their ceremonies would have been performed. It was that the great and glorious blaze of light from the mountain diamond would only take place after the last drop of the serpent's blood was spilled upon the Island, and that then the diamond itself would never again be found upon the rock where it had rested for so many ages. And I alone of them all knew this; but I knew not where the serpent was to be found. His influence was felt and seen, for in the early days he alone was the sole reptile that eluded pursuit, as his birth was due to the evil thoughts of a wandering black magician

28

who had landed for a week upon the Island so long before that the priests had no record of it. This serpent had to be killed and his blood spilled upon the ground to remove forever the last trace of the evil done by the magician, and for that event only was the diamond kept upon the mountain through the power of the good Adepts who had put it there. It preserved the germ of truth from the serpent's breath, and would not be needed when he was destroyed. Had the priests known this, no ceremonies for increasing its brilliancy would have been tried, as they would rather suffer the serpent's influence than lose the gem. Indeed, they believed that their tenure of power was in some way connected with the diamond mountain. They were right. I knew the fatal result for them when I succeeded in discovering the place of the serpent.

Day after day and long into the darkness of the night, I meditated and peered into every corner of the Island. At the full moon when the diamond grew a little clearer, I saw the slimy traces of the serpent upon the Island but could never find his lair. At last one night a fellow-student who had passed on before me with those by whom the diamond had been set, and who now and again returned through the aid to help his old friend, came to see me and, as he was going away, said, "Look at the foot of the mountain."

So near the sacred diamond I had never thought it possible the foul reptile could be found; and yet it was there, through the evil nature of the high- priest, he had taken up his secure retreat. I looked and saw him at the foot, breathing venom and black clouds of the soul's despair.

The great day of ceremonies for the diamond was again at hand, and I determined that then should witness the death of the serpent and the last bright shining of the diamond.

The morning broke clear and warm. Great throngs of people crowded about the mountain-temple, expectant of some great result from the ceremonies. It seemed as if these natural psychics felt within them that the diamond would burst forth with its ancient light, and yet every now and then a fear was expressed that in its greatest beauty it would be lost to them forever.

It was my turn to officiate at the ceremony after the high priest, and I alone was aware that the serpent had crawled even into the temple and was coiled up behind the shrine. I determined to seize him and, calling upon our ancient master, strangle him there and spill his blood upon the ground.

Even as I thought this, I saw my friend from other land enter the temple disguised as a wandering monk, and knew that my half-uttered aspiration even then was answered. Yet death stared me in the face. There, near the altar, was the sacred axe always ready to fell the man who in any way erred at the ceremony. This was one of the vile degenerations of the ancient law, and while it had been used before upon those who had only erred in the forms, I knew that the Priest himself would kill me as soon as the diamond's great flame had died away. The evening darkness would be upon us by the time that the moment in the performance permitted me to destroy the enemy of our race. So I cared not for death, for had I not faced it a thousand times as a blessed release and another chance.

At last the instant came. I stooped down, broke through the rule, and placing my hand behind the shrine caught the reptile by the neck. The High Priest saw me stoop and rushed to the axe. Another moment's delay, and all hope was gone. With superhuman power I grasped and squeezed. Through my skull shot a line of fire, and I could see my wandering monk wave his hand, and instantly the Priest stumbled and fell on his way to the axe. Another pressure, and the serpent was dead. My knife! It was in my girdle, and with it

I slit his neck. His red and lively blood poured out upon the ground and the axe fell upon my head, and the junior priest of the temple fell dead to the floor.

But only my body died. I rose upon the air and saw myself lying there. The people neither stirred nor spoke. The Priest bent over me. I saw my wandering monk smile. The serpent's blood spread slowly out beside my body, and then collected into little globes, each red and lively. The diamond on the mountain behind the temple slowly grew bright, then flashed and blazed. Its radiance penetrated the temple, while priests and people, except my wandering monk, prostrated themselves. Then sweet sounds and soft rustling filled the air, and voices in strange language spoke stranger words from the mountain. Yet still the people did not move. The light of the diamond seemed to gather around the serpent's blood. Slowly each globe of blood was eaten up by the light, except one more malevolent than the others, and then that fateful sphere of life rose up into the air, suddenly transformed itself into a small and spiteful snake that with undulating motion flew across the air and off into the night to the distant Isles. Priest and people arose in fear, the voices from the mountain ceased, the sounds died out, the light retreated, and darkness covered all. A wild cry of despair rose up into the night, and the priest rushed outside to look up at the mountain.

The serpent's blood still stained the ground, and the diamond had disappeared.

THE MAGIC SCREEN OF TIME

An old Hindu saying thus runs:

"He who knows that into which Time is resolved, knows all."

Time, in the Sanscrit, is called Kala. He is a destroyer and also a renovator. Yama, the lord of death, although powerful, is not so much so as Kala, for "until the time has come Yama can do nothing." The moments as they fly past before us carrying all things with them in long procession, are the atoms of Time, the sons of Kala. Years roll into centuries, centuries into cycles, and cycles become ages; but Time reigns over them all, for they are only his divisions.

Ah, for how many centuries have I seen Time, himself invisible, drawing pictures on his magic screen! When I saw the slimy trail of the serpent in the sacred Island of Destiny I knew not Time, for I thought the coming moment was different from the one I lived in, and both from that gone by. Nor then, either, did I know that that serpent instead of drawing his breath from the eternal ether, lived on the grossest form of matter; I saw not then how the flashing of the diamond set in the mountain was the eternal radiance of truth itself, but childishly fancied it had a beginning.

The tragedy in the temple, in which I was the victim — struck down by the high priest's axe, — was followed by another, as I found out soon when, freed from my body, I conversed in spirit with my friend the strange monk. He told me that the next day the high priest, upon recovering from the terrible event, went into the temple where my blood still stained the ground. The object of his visit was to gain time to meditate upon new plans for regaining his hold upon the people, which had been weakened by the blackening and disappearance of the mountain diamond. His thoughts dwelt upon the idea of manufacturing a substitute for the beautiful gem, but after remaining for a while plunged in such reveries his eye was attracted by a curious scene. Upon the stand from which he had snatched the axe that let out my life-blood he saw a cloud which seemed to be the end of a stream of vapour, rising up from the floor. Approaching, he perceived that my blood had in some curious way mixed with that which remained of the stains left by the reptile whose death I had accomplished, and from this the vapour arose, depositing itself, or collecting, upon the stand. And there to his amazement, in the centre of the cloud, he saw, slowly forming, a brilliant gem whose radiance filled the place.

"Ah, here" he cried, "is the diamond again. I will wait and see it fully restored, and then my triumph is complete. What seemed a murder will become a miracle."

As he finished the sentence the cloud disappeared, my blood was all taken up, and the flashing of the jewel filled him with Joy.

Reaching forth his hand he took it from the stand, and then black horror overspread his face. In vain he strove to move or to drop the gem; it seemed fastened to his hand; it grew smaller, and fiery pains shot through his frame. The other priests coming in just then to clear the place, stood fixed upon their steps at the door. The High Priest's face was toward them, and from his body came a flow of red and glittering light that shed fear over their hearts; nor could they move or speak. This lasted not long — only until the diamond had wholly disappeared from his hand — and then his frame split into a thousand pieces, while his accursed soul sped wailing through space accompanied by demoniacal shapes. The diamond was an illusion; it was my blood "crying from the ground," which took its shape from his thoughts and ambitions.

"Come then," said my monk, "come with me to the mountain."

We ascended the mountain in silence, and once at the top, he turned about fixing upon me a piercing gaze, under which I soon felt a sensation as if I was looking at a screen that hid something from my sight. The mountain and the monk disappeared and in their place I saw a city below me, for I was now upon the inner high tower of a very high building. It was an ancient temple dominating a city of magicians. Not far off was a tall and beautiful man: I knew it was my monk, but oh how changed; and near him stood a younger man from whom there seemed to reach out to me a steam of light, soft yet clear, thin yet plainly defined. I knew it was myself. Addressing my monk I said:

"What is this and why?"

"This is the past and the present," he replied; "and thou art the future."

"And he?" pointing to the young man. "That is thyself."

"How is it that I see this, and what holds it there?"

"'Tis the Magic Screen of Time, that holds it for thee and hides it ever. Look around and above thy head."

Obeying his command, I cast my eyes around the city spread below, and then looking upward I saw at first naught but the sky and the stars. But soon a surface appeared as if in the ether, through it shining still the stars, and then as my gaze grew steadfast the surface grew palpable and the stars went out; yet I knew instinctively that if my thoughts wandered for a moment the sky would once more fill the view. So I remained steady. Then slowly pictures formed upon the surface in the air. The city, its people, with all the colour of life; and a subdued hum appeared to float down from above as if the people were living up there. The scene wavered and floated away, and was succeeded by the thoughts and desires of those who lived below. No acts were there, but only lovely pictures formed by thoughts; living rainbows; flashing gems; pellucid crystals — until soon a dark and sinuous line crept through the dazzling view, with here and there black spots and lines. Then I heard the pleasing, penetrating voice of my monk:

"Time's screen rolls on; ambition, desire, jealousy, vanity, are defacing it. It will all soon fade. Watch."

And as I watched, centuries rolled past above me on the screen. Its beauty disappeared. Only a dark background with unpleasing and darker outlines of circumstances that surround contention and greed were offered to my eye. Here and there faint spots and lines of light were visible — the good deeds and thoughts of those still of spiritual mind. Then a question fell into my mind:

What is this screen?"

"It will be called the astral light when next you are born on earth," said the voice of my monk.

Just then a mighty sound of marching filled the space. The airy screen seemed to palpitate, its substance, if any it had, was pressed together, as if some oncoming force impinged upon it: its motion grew tumultuous; and then the stars once more shone down from the sky, and I hovered in spirit on the dark mountain where the gem had been. No beings were near, but from the distant spaces came a voice that said,

"Listen to the march of the Future."

THE WANDERING EYE

This is not a tale in which I fable a mythical and impossible monster such as the Head of Rahu, which the common people of India believe swallows the moon at every eclipse. Rahu is but a tale that for the vulgar embodies the fact that the shadow of the earth eats up the white disc, but I tell you of a vertable human eye; a wanderer, a seeker, a pleader; an eye that searched you out and held you, like the fascinated bird by the serpent, while it sought within your nature for what it never found. Such an eye as this is sometimes spoken of now by various people, but they see it on the psychic plane, in the astral light, and it is not to be seen or felt in the light of day moving about like other objects.

This wandering eye I write of was always on the strange and sacred Island where so many things took place long ages ago. Ah! yes, it is still the sacred Island, now obscured and its power overthrown — some think forever. But its real power will be spiritual, and as the minds of men to-day know not the spirit, caring only for temporal glory, the old virtue of the Island will once again return. What weird and ghostly shapes still flit around her shores; what strange, low, level, whisperings sweep across her mountains; how at the evening's edge just parted from the day, her fairies suddenly remembering their human rulers — now sunk to men who partly fear them — gather for a moment about the sports where mystery is buried, and then sighing speed away. It was here the wandering eye was first seen. By day it had simply a grey colour, piercing, steady, and always bent on finding out some certain thing from which it could not be diverted; at night it glowed with a light of its own, and could be seen moving over the Island, now quickly, now slowly as it settled to look for that which it did not find.

The people had a fear of this eye, although they were then accustomed to all sorts of magical occurrences now unknown to most western men. At first those who felt themselves annoyed by it tried to destroy or catch it, but never succeeded, because the moment they made the attempt the eye would disappear. It never manifested resentment, but seemed filled with a definite purpose and bent toward a well settled end. Even those who had essayed to do away with it were surprised to find no threatening in its depth when, in the darkness of the night, it floated up by their bedsides and looked them over again.

If anyone else save myself knew of the occasion when this marvelous wanderer first started, to whom it had belonged, I never heard. I was bound to secrecy and could not reveal it.

In the same old temple and tower to which I have previously referred, there was an old man who had always been on terms of great intimacy with me. He was a disputer and a doubter, yet terribly in earnest and anxious to know the truths of nature, but continually raised the question: "If I could only know the truth; that is all I wish to know.

Then, whenever I suggested solutions received from my teachers, he would wander away to the eternal doubts. The story was whispered about the temple that he had entered life in that state of mind, and was known to the superior as one who, in a preceding life, had raised doubts and impossibilities merely for the sake of hearing solutions without desire to prove anything, and had vowed, after many years of such profitless discussion, to seek for truth alone. But the Karma accumulated by the lifelong habit had not been exhausted, and in the incarnation when I met him, although sincere and earnest, he was hampered by the pernicious habit of the previous life.

Hence the solutions he sought were always near but ever missed.

But toward the close of the life of which I am speaking he obtained a certainty that by peculiar practices he could concentrate in his eye not only the sight but also all the other forces, and wilfully set about the task against my strong protest. Gradually his eyes assumed a most extraordinary and piercing expression which was heightened whenever he indulged in discussion. He was hugging the one certainty to his breast and still suffering from the old Karma of doubt. So he fell sick, and being old came near to death. One night I visited him at his request, and on reaching his side I found him approaching dissolution. We were alone. He spoke freely but very sadly, for, as death drew near, he saw more clearly, and as the hours fled by his eyes grew more extraordinarily piercing than ever, with a pleading, questioning expression.

"Ah," he said, "I have erred again; but it is just Karma. I have succeeded in but one thing, and that ever will delay me."

"What is that?" I asked.

The expression of his eyes seemed to embrace futurity as he told me that his peculiar practice would compel him for a long period to remain chained to his strongest eye the right one — until the force of the energy expended in learning that one feat was fully exhausted. I saw death slowly creeping over his features, and when I had thought him dead he suddenly gained strength to make me promise not to reveal the secret — and expired.

As he passed away, it was growing dark. After his body had become cold, there in the darkness I saw a human eye glowing and gazing at me. It was his, for I recognized the expression. All his peculiarities and modes of thought seemed fastened into it sweeping out over you from it. Then it turned from me, soon disappearing. His body was buried; none save myself and our superiors knew of these things. But for many years afterwards the wandering eye was seen in every part of the Island, ever seeking, ever asking and never waiting for the answer.

THE TELL-TALE PICTURE GALLERY

Although the gallery of pictures about which I now write has long ago been abandoned, and never since its keepers left the spot where it was has it been seen there, similar galleries are still to be found in places that one cannot get into until guided to them. They are now secreted in distant and inaccessible spots; in the Himalaya mountains, beyond them, in Tibet, in underground India, and such mysterious localities. The need for reports by spies or for confessions by transgressors is not felt by secret fraternities which possess such strange recorders of the doings, thoughts, and condition of those whom they portray. In the brotherhoods of the Roman Catholic Church or in Freemasonry, no failure to abide by rules could ever be dealt with unless some one reported the delinquent or he himself made a confession. Every day mason after mason breaks both letter and spirit of the vows he made, but, no one knowing or making charges, he remains a mason in good standing. The soldier in camp or field oversteps the strictest rules of discipline, yet if done out of sight of those who could divulge or punish he remains untouched. And in the various religious bodies, the members continually break, either in act or in thought, all the commandments, unknown to their fellows and the heads of the Church, with no loss of standing. But neither the great Roman Church, the Freemasons, nor any religious sect possesses such a gallery as that of which I will try to tell you, one in which is registered every smallest deed and thought.

I do not mean the great Astral Light that retains faithful pictures of all we do, whether we be Theosophists or Scoffers, Catholics or Freemasons, but a vertable collection of simulacra deliberately constructed so as to specialise one of the many functions of the Astral Light.

It was during one of my talks with the old man who turned into a wandering eye that I first heard of this wonderful gallery, and after his death I was shown the place itself. It was kept on the Sacred Island where of old many weird and magical things existed and events occurred. You may ask why these are not now found there, but you might as well request that I explain why Atlantis sank beneath the wave or why the great Assyrian Empire has disappeared. They have had their day, just as our present boasted civilization will come to its end and be extinguished. Cyclic law cannot be held from its operation, and just as sure as tides change on the globe and blood flows in the body, so sure is it that great doings reach their conclusion and powerful nations disappear.

It was only a few months previous to the old man's death, when approaching dissolution or superior orders, I know not which, caused him to reveal many things and let slip hints as to others. He had been regretting his numerous errors one day, and turning to me said,

"And have you never seen the gallery where your actual spiritual state records itself?"

Not knowing what he meant I replied, "I did not know they had one here."

"Oh yes; it is in the old temple over by the mountain, and the diamond gives more light there than anywhere else."

Fearing to reveal my dense ignorance, not only of what he meant but also of the nature of this gallery, I continued the conversation in a way to elicit more information, and he, supposing I had known of others, began to describe, this one. But in the very important part of the description he turned the subject as quickly as he had introduced it, so, that I remained a prey to curiosity. And until the day of his death he did not again refer to it. The extraordinary manner of his decease, followed by the weird wandering eye, drove the thought of the pictures out of my head.

But it would seem that the effect of this floating, lonely, intelligent eye upon my character was a shadow or foretoken of my introduction to the gallery. His casual question, in connection with his own shortcomings and the lesson impressed on me by the intensification and concentration of all his nature into one eye that ever wandered about the Island, made me turn my thoughts inward so as to discover and destroy the seeds of evil in myself. Meanwhile all duties in the temple where I lived were assiduously performed. One night after attaining to some humility of spirit, I fell quietly asleep with the white moonlight falling over the floor and dreamed that I met the old man again as when alive, and that he asked me if I had yet seen the picture gallery. "No," said I in the dream, "I had forgotten it," awakening then at sound of my own voice. Looking up, I saw standing in the moonlight a figure of one I had not seen in any of the temples. This being gazed at me with clear, cold eyes, and far off sounded what I supposed its voice,

"Come with me."

Rising from the bed I went out into the night, following this laconic guide. The moon was full, high in her course, and all the place was full of her radiance. In the distance the walls of the temple nearest the diamond mountain appeared self-luminous. To that the guide walked, and we reached the door now standing wide open. As I came to the threshold, suddenly the lonely, grey, wandering eye of my old dead friend and co- disciple floated past looking deep into my own, and I read its expression as if it would say,

"The picture gallery is here."

We entered, and, although some priests were there, no one seemed to notice me. Through a court, across a hall, down a long corridor we went, and then into a wide and high roofless place with but one door. Only the stars in heaven adorned the space above, while streams of more than moonlight poured into it from the diamond, so that there were no shadows nor any need for lights. As the noiseless door swung softly to behind us, sad music floated down the place and ceased; just then a sudden shadow seemed to grow in one spot, but was quickly swallowed in the light.

"Examine with care, but touch not and fear nothing," said my taciturn cicerone. With these words he turned and let me alone.

But how could I say I was alone? The place was full of faces. They were ranged up and down the long hall; near the floor, above it, higher, on the walls, in the air, everywhere except in one aisle, but not a single one moved from its place, yet each was seemingly alive. And at intervals strange watchful creatures of the elemental world that moved about from place to place. Were they watching me or the faces? Now I felt they had me in view, for sudden glances out of the corners of their eyes shot my way; but in a moment something happened showing they guarded or watched the faces.

I was standing looking at the face of an old friend about my own age who had been sent to another part of the island, and it filled me with sadness unaccountably. One of the curious elemental creatures moved silently up near it. In amazement I strained my eyes, for the picture of my friend was apparently discolouring. Its expression altered every moment. It turned from white to grey and yellow, and back to grey, and then suddenly it grew all black as if with rapid decomposition. Then again that same sad music I had heard on entering floated past me, while the blackness of the face seemed to cast a shadow, but not long. The elemental pounced upon the blackened face now soulless, tore it in pieces, and by some

44

process known to itself dissipated the atoms and restored the brightness of the spot. But alas! my old friend's picture was gone, and I felt within me a heavy, almost unendurable gloom as of despair.

As I grew accustomed to the surroundings, my senses perceived every now and then sweet but low musical sounds that appeared to emanate from or around these faces. So, selecting one, I stood in front of it and watched. It was bright and pure. Its eyes looked into mine with the half-intelligence of a dream. Yes, it grew now and then a little brighter, and as that happened I heard the gentle music. This convinced me that the changes in expression were connected with the music.

But fearing I would be called away, I began to carefully scan the collection, and found that all my co-disciples were represented there, as well as hundreds whom I had never seen, and every priest high or low whom I had observed about the island. Yet the same saddening music every now and then reminded me of the scene of the blackening of my friend's picture. I knew it meant others blackened and being destroyed by the watchful elementals who I could vaguely perceive were pouncing upon something whenever those notes sounded. They were like the wails of angels when they see another mortal going to moral suicide.

Dimly after a while there grew upon me an explanation of this gallery. Here were the living pictures of every student or priest of the order founded by the Adepts of the Diamond Mountain. These vitalized pictures were connected by invisible cords with the character of those they represented, and like a telegraph instrument they instantly recorded the exact state of the disciple's mind; when he made a complete failure, they grew black and were destroyed; when he progressed in spiritual life, their degrees of brightness or beauty showed his exact standing. As these conclusions were

45

reached, louder and stronger musical tones filled the hall. Directly before me was a beautiful, peaceful face; its brilliance outshone the light around, and I knew that some unseen brother — how far or near was unknown to me — had reached some height of advancement that corresponded to such tones. Just then my guide reentered; I found I was near the door; it was open, and together we passed out, retracing the same course by which we had entered. Outside again the setting of the moon showed how long I had been in the gallery. The silence of my guide prevented speech, and he returned with me to the room I had left. There he stood looking at me, and once more I heard as it were from afar his voice in inquiry, as if he said but

"Well?"

Into my mind came the question "How are those faces made?" From all about him, but not from his lips came the answer,

"You cannot understand. They are not the persons, and yet they are made from their minds and bodies."

"Was I right in the idea that they were connected with those they pictured by invisible cords along which the person's condition was carried?"

"Yes, perfectly. And they never err. From day to day they change for better or for worse. Once the disciple has entered this path his picture forms there; and we need no spies, no officious fellow disciples to prefer charges, no reports, no machinery. Everything registers itself. We have but to inspect the images to know just how the disciple gets on or goes back."

"And those curious elementals," thought I, "do they feed on the blackened images?"

"They are our scavengers. They gather up and dissipate the decomposed and deleterious atoms that formed the image before it grew black — no longer fit for such good company."

"And the music, — did it come from the images?"

"Ah, boy, you have much to learn. It came from them, but it belongs also to every other soul. It is the vibration of the disciple's thoughts and spiritual life; it is the music of his good deeds and his brotherly love."

Then there came to me a dreadful thought, "How can one — if at all — restore his image once it has blackened in the gallery?"

But my guide was no longer there. A faint rustling sound was all — and three deep far notes as if upon a large bronze bell!

THE SKIN OF THE EARTH

The cold materialism of the 19th century paralyzes sentiment and kills mysticism. Thus it commits a double crime, in robbing man and preventing many classes of sentient beings from progressing up the ladder that leads from earth to heaven. So in telling these tales I feel sheltered behind the shield of the editor of the magazine for which I write, for, were I to be known as believing that any beings whatever other than man are affected by the mental negations of the century, my life would soon become a burden. This age is so full of ignorance that it sees not and cares nothing for the groans that are rolling among the caverns of mother earth fathoms deep below its surface. Nor will it care until its contempt for what it calls superstition shall have caused its ruin, and then — another age will have risen and other men have come.

It was not so in our Sacred Island cycles ago. Then what we call superstition was knowledge that has now been replaced by impudent scorn for aught save the empiric classification of a few facts; a heritage of glory given up for a mere statement of the limits of our ignorance. But I will plunge into the past and forget the present hour.

Seven months had rolled away since the time when, standing in the picture gallery, I had seen the simulacrum of a dear friend blacken and disappear, and now on the morning of the day when I was to pass by the mountain of the diamond, the news was brought to me how head fallen faithless to his trust overcome by vanity with its dark companion, doubt.

So, at the appointed hour I waited for the messenger. Once again the white moonbeams shone into the room and, revealing the monthly dial curiously wrought into the floor and walls by a chemical art that allowed nothing to be revealed save by moonlight after the 14th day of her course, told me in a language pale and cold that this was the 17th day. I stood and watched the dial, fascinated by the symbols that crept out with the silvery light, although for years I had seen the same thing every month. But now as I looked some new combination of our ancient magic was revealed. Every now and then clouds seemed to roll across the floor, while on them rested the earth itself. This I had never seen before. Seven times it rolled by, and then I felt that near me stood the silent messenger. Turning I saw him just as he stood when he called me to the gallery.

"Do you not know this picture?" said he. "No. All is dark to me."

"It is the sign that you are to come to the earth's hall beyond the gallery. Look again closely at that rolling ball upon the clouds, and tell me what you see."

These words seemed to come not from the man's lips, but from all about him, as if the air was full of sound. But obeying the direction I gazed at the picture and saw that the surface of the mystic globe was moving, and then that myriads of small creatures were coming through it.

"It is time," said the sounds from all about the impassive being. "That is the signal. We will go;" And he turned away.

I followed while he led me up to the building and through the gallery of tell-tale pictures where still in the silence the faces changed and the soft music sounded. I would have lingered there to see those magic pictures, but a cord seemed to draw me after my guide. As we approached the other end of the gallery nothing was visible to the eye save a blank wall, but the messenger passed through it and disappeared. Afraid to stop, unable to resist the drawing of the

50

invisible cord, I walked against the wall. One short moment of suspense and with my breath held I had passed through; it was but a cloud, or a vapour — and I was on the other side. Turning expecting to still see through that immaterial wall, I found that it was impervious to the sight, and then the cord that drew me slackened, for my guide had stopped. Stepping up to the wall, my outstretched fingers went through it, or rather disappeared within it, for they felt no sensation. Then the messenger's voice said,

"Such is the skin of the Earth to those who live below it." With these words he walked on again through a door of a large room into which I followed. Here a faint but oppressive smell of earth filled all the space, and, standing just inside the door-way now closed by a noiselessly moving door, I saw that the whole place save where we stood was moving, as if the great globe were here seen revolving upon its axis and all its motions felt.

As I gazed the surface of the revolving mass was seen to be covered with circling hosts of small creatures whose movements caused the revolutions, and all at once it seemed as if the moving body became transparent, and within was filled with the same creatures. They were constantly coming from the surface and moving to the centre along well-defined paths. Here was the whole globe represented in forcible miniature, and these creatures within and upon it of their own nature moved it, guided by some mysterious Being whose presence was only revealed by beams of light. Nor could the others see him, but his silent directions were carried out.

These little beings were of every colour and form; some wore an appearance similar to that of man himself, others appeared like star blossoms of the sea, their pure tints waxing and waning as they throbbed with an interior pulse of light. Whatever their shapes, these seemed evanescent, translucent, and easily dissipated; in their real

51

essence the creatures were centres of energy, a nucleolus around which light condensed, now in this form, now in that, with constant progression of type and form. Some were more swift and harmonious in their movements than others, and these I understood were the more progressed in the scale of Being. Such had a larger orbit, and satellites circled about them. Of such systems the place was full, and all owned obedience to the subtle and interior Power which I could not, discern. Each system existed for the service of all the rest; each complemented and sustained the others as they swept onward in a harmony that was labour and love. Their object seemed twofold; they assisted in maintaining the revolutions of the earth upon its axis and in guiding it in its orbit. They also grew through the ever-increasing swiftness of their own motions into greater splendour and brightness, approaching greater intelligence, coming ever nearer to self-conscious reason and love, and, as they grew, stimulated the latent spark in the metals and all the underworld growth as the lambent touch of flame awakens flame.

Guided by the Unseen Power and in their automatic obedience (for to obey was their nature), there were some who by the greatness of their own momentum and the ferment of new forces attracted and gathering about them, seemed upon the point of bursting into some fuller expansion, some higher state of intelligence and life, but they were withheld by something that was not the Power guiding them. Looking closer, I saw that an antagonistic influence was at work in the place.

The orbit of many of these docile and beautiful creatures included a passage to and fro through the mystic wall. Their duties were upon the earth as well as beneath its surface; faithful fulfilment of these functions comprised an evolution into higher service and a higher form. The malign influence often prevented this. It seemed like a dark mist full of noxious vapour that deadened while it chilled.

As the clouds rolled into the hall their wreaths assumed now this shape and now that, changeful and lurid suggestions of hatred, lust, and pride. Many of the creatures coming in contact with these had that influence stamped upon their sensitive spheres, giving them the horrid likeness which they were powerless to shake off, and thus becoming servants of the baleful mist itself with altered and discordant motions. Others were paralyzed with the chill contact. Others were so taxed to make up for the partial suspension of their fellows' activity that their work was unsteady and their orbital revolutions checked. But still the whole throng swung on like some splendid creation, paling, glowing, throbbing, pausing, a huge iridescent heart scintillating, singing through the gloom. Here the mist was beaten back by greater efforts that jarred the harmony; there it gathered, condensed, and in its vile embrace swept in bright systems, stifling their motions, then leaving them paralyzed where they fell, while it crawled on to fresh victims. And all through this strange picture and wonderful battle I could see the dim cloud-like shapes of cities inhabited by the men of earth, my fellows, and also the rivers, mountains, and trees of the globe.

In my mind the query rose, "Why do the earth's cities look like dreams?"

And there upon the wall flashed out this sentence, while its meaning sounded in every letter:

"When you are being shown the elemental beings, the men of your earth and their cities appear as clouds because it is not to them that your mind is directed. Look yet again!

I saw that the evil mist had gathered strength in one part of the place, and had destroyed the harmony and swiftness of so many of the little beings that the great circling globe was moving off its axis, circling more and more, so that I knew upon whatever earth this happened great changes would occur, and that in the path of the mist there would sweep over man epidemics of disease and crime. Horrified at such impending calamities I sought for an answer and looked towards my guide. As I did so he disappeared, and upon the wall his voice seemed to paint itself in living letters that themselves gave out a sound.

"*It is the thoughts of men.*" I hid my face, appalled at owning such a heritage, and when I looked again great jets spurted through the Skin of the Earth, thoughts spouting and pouring out in miasmatic streams.

I would have asked much more, but again from some vast distance came the tones of the deep bronze bell; a shower of earth's blossoms fell about me; I had passed the wall; my guide was gone; and I was alone in my own room reflecting on what I had seen.

TRUE PROGRESS

Perhaps those who have engaged in discussions about whether it is more advisable to become acquainted with the Astral Plane and to see therein than to study the metaphysics and ethics of theosophy, may be aided by the experience of a fellow student. For several years I studied about and experimented on the Astral Light to the end that I might, if possible, develop the power to look therein and see those marvellous pictures of that plane which tempt the observer. But although in some degree success followed my efforts so far as seeing these strange things was concerned, I found no increase of knowledge as to the manner in which the pictures were made visible, nor as to the sources from which they rose. A great many facts were in my possession, but the more I accumulated the farther away from perception seemed the law governing them. I turned to a teacher, and he said:

"Beware of the illusions of matter."

"But," said I, "is this matter into which I gaze?"

"Yes; and of grosser sort than that which composes your body; full of illusions, swarming with beings inimical to progress, and crowded with the thoughts of all the wicked who have lived."

"How," replied I, "am I to know aught about it unless I investigate it?"

"It will be time enough to do that when you shall have been equipped properly for the exploration. He who ventures into a strange country unprovided with needful supplies, without a compass and unfamiliar with the habits of the people, is in danger. Examine and see."

Left thus to myself, I sought those who had dabbled in the Astral Light, who were accustomed to seeing the pictures therein every day, and asked them to explain. Not one had any theory, any philosophical basis. All were confused and at variance each with the other. Nearly all, too, were in hopeless ignorance as to other and vital questions. None were self- contained or dispassionate; moved by contrary winds of desire, each one appeared abnormal; for, while in possession of the power to see or hear in the Astral Light, they were unregulated in all other departments of their being. Still more, they seemed to be in a degree intoxicated with the strangeness of the power, for it placed them in that respect above other persons, yet in practical affairs left them without any ability.

Examining more closely, I found that all these "seers" were but half-seers — and hardly even that. One could hear astral sounds but could not see astral sights; another saw pictures, but no sound or smell was there; still others saw symbols only, and each derided the special power of the other. Turning even to the great Emanuel Swedenborg, I found a seer of wonderful power, but whose constitution made him see in the Astral world a series of pictures which were solely an extension of his own inherited beliefs And although he had had a few visions of actual everyday affairs occurring at a distance, they were so few as only to be remarkable.

One danger warned against by the teacher was then plainly evident. It was the danger of becoming confused and clouded in mind by the recurrence of pictures which had no salutary effect so far as experience went. So again I sought the teacher and asked:

"Has the Astral Light no power to teach and, if not, why is it thus? And are there other dangers than what I have discovered?"

"No power whatever has the astral plane, in itself, to teach you. It contains the impressions made by men in their ignorance and folly. Unable to arouse the true thoughts, they continue to infect that light with the virus of their unguided lives. And you, or any other seer, looking therein will warp and distort all that you find there. It will present to you pictures that partake largely of your own constitutional habits, weaknesses, and peculiarities. Thus you only see a distorted or exaggerated copy of yourself. It will never teach you the reason of things, for it knows them not.

"But stranger dangers than any you have met are there when one goes further on. The dweller of the threshold is there, made up of all the evil that man has done. None can escape its approach, and he who is not prepared is in danger of death, of despair, or of moral ruin. Devote, yourself, therefore, to spiritual aspiration and to true devotion, which will be a means for you to learn the causes that operate in nature, how they work, and what each one works upon."

I then devoted myself as he had directed, and discovered that a philosophical basis, once acquired, showed clearly how to arrive at *dispassion* and made *exercise* therein easy. It even enables me to clear up the thousand doubts that assail those others who are peering into the Astral Light. This too is the old practice enjoined by the ancient schools from which our knowledge about the Astral Light is derived. They compelled the disciple to abjure all occult practices until such time as he had laid a sure foundation of logic, philosophy, and ethics; and only then was he permitted to go further in that strange country from which many an unprepared explorer has returned bereft of truth and sometimes despoiled of reason. Further, I know that the Masters of the Theosophical Society have written these words: "Let the Theosophical Society flourish through moral worth and philosophy, and give up pursuit of phenomena." Shall we be greater than They, and ignorantly set the pace upon the path that leads to ruin?

WHERE THE RISHIS WERE

The rishis were the sacred Bards, the Saints, the great Adepts known to the Hindus, who gave great spiritual impulses in the past and are said to sometimes reincarnate, and who at one time lived on earth among men.

The world is made of seas and islands. For continents are only great lands water-encircled. Men must ever live upon sea or land, then, unless they abide in air, and if they live in the air they are not men as we know them." Thus I thought as the great ship steamed slowly into the port of a small island, and before the anchor fell the whole scene seemed to change and the dazzling light of the past blotted out the dark pictures of modern civilization. Instead of an English ship I was standing on an ancient vehicle propelled by force unknown today, until the loud noises of disembarkation roused me once again.

But landed now and standing on the hill overlooking the town and bay, the strange light, the curious vehicle again obtained mastery over sense and eye, while the whole majesty of forgotten years rolled in from the ocean. Vainly did modern education struggle and soar: I let the curtain drop upon the miserable present.

Now softly sings the water as it rolls against the shore, with the sun but one hour old shining upon its surface. But far off, what is that spot against the sky coming nearer from the West, followed by another and another until over the horizon rise hundreds, and now some are so near that they are plainly seen? The same strange vehicles as that I saw at first. Like birds they fly through the air. They come slowly now, and some have been brought still on the land. They light on the earth with a softness that seems nearly human, with a skill that is marvellous, without any shock or rebound. From them there alight men of noble mien who address me as friends, and one more noble than the others seems to say, "wouldst thou know of all this? Then come," as he turns again to his vehicle that stands there like a bird in wait to be off.

"Yes, I will go;" and I felt that the past and the present were but one, and knew what I should see, yet could not remember it but with a vagueness that blotted out all the details.

We entered the swift, intelligently-moving vehicle, and then it rose up on the air's wide-spreading arms and flew again fast to the west whence it had come. It passed many more flying east to the Island, where the water was, still softly singing to the beams of the sun. The horizon slowly rose and the Island behind us was hidden by sea from our sight. And still as onward we flew to the occident, many more birds made by man like that we were in flew by us as if in haste for the soft-singing water lapping the shore of that peak of the sea-mountain we had left in the Orient. Flying too high at first, we heard no sound from the sea, but soon a damp vapor that blew in my face from the salt deep showed that we were descending and then spoke my friend.

"Look below and around and before you!"

Down there were the roar and the rush of mad billows that reached toward the sky, vast hollows that sucked in a world. Black clouds shut out the great sun, and I saw that the crust of the earth was drawn in to her own subterranean depths. Turning now to the master, I saw that he, heard my unuttered question. He said:

"A cycle has ended. The great bars that kept back the sea have broken down by their weight. From these we have come and are coming."

Then faster sailed our bird, and I saw that a great Island was perishing. What was left of the shore still crumbled, still entered the mouth of the sea. And there were cars of the air just the same as that I was in, only, dark and unshining, vainly trying to rise with their captains; rising slowly, then falling, and then swallowed up.

But here we have rushed further in where the water has not overflowed, and now we see that few are the bright cars of air that are waiting about while their captains are entering and spoiling the mighty dark cars of the men whose clothing is red and whose bodies, so huge and amazing, are sleeping as if from the fumes of a drug.

As these great red men are slumbering, the light-stepping captains with sun- colored cloaks are finishing the work of destruction. And now, swiftly though we came, the waters have rushed on behind us, the salt breath of the all-devouring deep sweeps over us. The sun-colored captains enter their light air-cars and rise with a sweep that soon leaves the sleepers, now waking, behind them. The huge red-coated giants hear the roar of the waters and feel the cold waves roll about them. They enter their cars, but only to find all their efforts are wasted. Soon the crumbling earth no longer supports them, and all by an in-rushing wave are engulfed, drawn into the mouth of the sea, and the treacherous ocean with roars as of pleasure in conquest has claimed the last trace of the Island.

But one escaped of all the red giants, and slowly but surely his car sailed up, up, as if to elude the sun-colored men who were spoilers.

Then loud, clear, and thrilling swelled out a note of marvelous power from my captain, and back came a hundred of those brilliant, fast cars that were speeding off eastward. Now they pursue the heavy, vast, slow-moving ear of the giants surround it, and seem to avoid its attacks. Then again swells that note from my master as our car hung still on its wings. It was a signal, obeyed in an instant.

One brilliant, small, sharp-pointed car is directed full at the red giant's vehicle. Propelled by a force that exceeds the swift bullet, it pierces the other; itself, too, is broken and falls on the wave with its victim. Trembling, I gaze down below, but my captain said kindly,

"He is safe, for he entered another bright car at the signal. All those red- coated men are now gone, and that last was the worst and the greatest."

Back eastward once more through the salt spray and the mist until soon the bright light shone again and the Island rose over the sea with the soft- singing water murmuring back to the sun. We alighted, and then, as I turned, the whole fleet of swift-sailing cars disappeared, and out in the sky there flashed a bright streak of sun-colored light that formed into letters which read,

"This is where the Rishis were before the chalk cliffs of Albion rose out of the wave. They were but are not."

And loud, clear, and thrilling rose that note I had heard in the car of swift pinions. It thrilled me with sadness, for past was the glory and naught for the future was left but a destiny.

THE COMING OF THE SERPENT

The white rays shed over all the Island when the Diamond on the mountain shot forth its last light continued shining until the malignant snake formed from the serpent's blood had fled all across the sea and reached the great Isle beyond. Then all became black as night to the people. Deprived of my body that lay cold and dead beside the altar, I could see the high priest bending over the corpse until the growing darkness filled him with alarm which changed to terror. As he rose from his bending attitude I heard a solemn voice that filled all the space around utter these words:

"The cycle is ended. Thou hast completed a part of thy work, leaving a little in the new malignant snake to be done. Thou must follow it to the other Islands until fate shall lead thee elsewhere. Fear not but proceed with a calm courage, for we are ever beside thee, the same in the dark as in the light."

A sudden faintness filled my ethereal body, shadowy forms flitted about me, and I knew I was flying eastward with the vast heaving sea below me.

On and on I fled and soon perceived the smell of earth. Over the other Island to the west I was floating in an atmosphere loaded with heavy emanations. I lost consciousness — and then I was born in another land, in the Island to the East, and even as a child I knew that the serpent's blood had come before me, knew full well I should meet it some day.

In time I entered in company with the Druids, and one of them told of the coming of the serpent.

My teacher and narrator was a tall old man, over a century in age. A long white beard fell over his breast. Large blue eyes that seemed alive with a light of their own showed his soul gazing at you, but they were strong and fearless in expression. They pierced your being, but carried calmness and hope with them.

A calmness born from many lives of struggle and triumph, a hope arising from a vast and comprehensive view of the future; for he was a seer and knew the coming and going of the great tides of time. He said:

"Boy, your questions grow out of experience in the past. The serpent is in this land. Here we came long, long ago, after many centuries of watching, from the shore of the Island of the Diamond, while this land slowly rose up from the deep to touch the surface of the water and then emerge. For your own island is far older than this. We planted huge stones of magic potency in the slime as it came near the surface, and held them in place by the same power, hoping to prepare in advance for the Serpent which we knew was to come. But human hearts and wills alone can conquer: magic stones and amulets and charms subserve but a temporary end. Many centuries passed thus, and after the land had arisen, became clothed with vegetation and inhabited by people, we sorrowfully saw the emanations from colonists were thickening day by day.

"Across the sea the Diamond Mountain threw up over the horizon a faint and beautiful light by night, a bluish haze by day. Then one night as with my brothers I sat looking westward, the light on the sky blazed up with sudden force. We knew the hour had come. The darkness fell greater as that holy light faded away, and through the air a hissing sound came across the sea. It was the serpent's blood, one drop changed into a smaller snake that flew from the west. That was the day you violated rules, throttled the ancient serpent behind the altar, and lost your life at the hands of the high-priest of a false, a counterfeit religion.

"In vain our chants arose around the mighty stones that stood majestically in the plain. On and on, louder and louder, came that malignant hiss; down on the ground, even close to the stones of the Sun, fell the serpent and disappeared from our sight.

"Since then its baleful influence has been felt over all the land, and until thy coming we knew not when any deliverer should arise. In thee is locked up the power to destroy the last remnants of the power of the serpent's blood. Perhaps thy ancient friends will help, for although thou art younger here, yet thou art older than we all. Be wise and true. Forget no duty, omit no effort, and one day the last drop of that ephidian blood will be altered by thy power and art, will be transmuted into elixir."

AN ALLEGORY

Walking within the garden of his heart, the pupil suddenly came upon the Master, and was glad, for he had but just finished a task in His service which he hastened to lay at His feet.

"See, Master," said he, "this is done: now give me other teaching to do." The Master looked upon him sadly yet indulgently, as one might upon a child

which can not understand.

"There are already many to teach intellectual conceptions of the Truth," he replied. "Thinkest thou to serve best by adding thyself to their number?"

The pupil was perplexed.

"Ought we not to proclaim the Truth from the very housetops, until the whole world shall have heard?" he asked.

"And then — "

"Then the whole world will surely accept it."

"Nay," replied the Master, "the Truth is not of the intellect, but of the heart. See!"

The pupil looked, and saw the Truth as though it were a White Light, flooding the whole earth; yet none reaching the green and living plants which so sorely needed its rays, because of dense layers of clouds intervening.

"The clouds are the human intellect," said the Master. "Look again."

Intently gazing, the pupil saw here and there faint rifts in the clouds, through which the Light struggled in broken, feeble beams. Each rift was caused by a little vortex of vibrations, and looking down through the openings thus made the pupil perceived that each vortex had its origin in a human heart.

"Only by adding to and enlarging the rifts will the Light ever reach the earth," said the Master. "Is it best, then, to pour out more Light upon the clouds, or to establish a vortex of heart force? The latter thou must accomplish unseen and unnoticed and even unthanked. The former will bring thee praise and notice among men, Both are necessary: both are Our work; but — the rifts are so few! Art strong enough to forego the praise and make of thyself a heart centre of pure impersonal force?"

The pupil sighed, for it was a sore question.